THE
TWELVE APOSTLES
THEIR LIVES AND ACTS
Marianna Mayer

Phyllis Fogelman Books · New York

In loving memory of Sister Maria Fidelis,
mentor and friend

Published by Phyllis Fogelman Books
An imprint of Penguin Putnam Books for Young Readers
345 Hudson Street
New York, New York 10014

Copyright © 2000 by Marianna Mayer
All rights reserved
Designed by Marianna Mayer and Atha Tehon
The text for this book is set in Centaur.
Printed in Hong Kong on acid-free paper
1 3 5 7 9 10 8 6 4 2
Library of Congress Cataloging-in-Publication Data
available upon request

Author's Note

Jesus instilled in his apostles devotion to one single task: to announce the Good News—the coming kingdom of God. The word apostle comes from the Greek *apostolos,* meaning "one who is sent out." The apostles abandoned all else—home, wife, parents, children—for the sake of this mission, and not one looked back to his old life with regret. Sharing the nomadic way of life with Jesus—living in poverty, carrying no money, accepting any hospitality offered—permitted them to attend unhindered to their task as his chosen messengers. Jesus said to the apostles, "Whoever welcomes you welcomes me, and whoever welcomes me welcomes the one who sent me."[1]

The gospels record that Jesus had many disciples, from whom he chose a dozen to be his select members. To this group, called "the Twelve," Jesus gave the power to cast out evil, to heal, and to preach his teachings. Their number corresponds to that of the twelve tribes of ancient Israel. A deliberate choice, for Jesus promised the Twelve that their reward, at the time of reckoning, would be to sit on twelve thrones and to judge the twelve tribes.[2]

The list of those who comprised the Twelve appear in all three synoptic gospels: Matthew 10:2-4; Mark 3:16-19; Luke 6:13-16. The lists are basically identical: Peter/Simon (also called Cephas) and his brother Andrew; James and John, the sons of Zebedee; Philip; Bartholomew (who may be called Nathanael in John's gospel); Matthew (or Levi) the tax collector; Thomas Didymus ("the Twin"); James, the son of Alphaeus; Simon the Zealot; Thaddaeus, variously called Lebbaeus or the son of James; and Judas Iscariot. The Twelve were a fixed and unchanging group that remained closest to Jesus, until the death of Judas Iscariot. After his death, the number had to be maintained by choosing someone who had accompanied Jesus throughout his entire ministry;[3] thus Matthias was appointed. Until their deaths, the new Twelve continued to carry out Jesus' work.

Peter

Holy Scripture names Peter the first of all the apostles, though Peter, a humble fisherman, never put himself first. In many ways the holy apostle is most like us, for his complex nature reveals him to be very human; he is passionate and loyal, cowardly and courageous.

Once called Simon, he was given the name Peter [meaning *rock*] by Jesus, who said of him, "Upon this rock I will build my church."[4]

Jesus also told Peter at the Last Supper that he would deny him. Peter loved his master, yet that night, after Jesus' arrest by the temple soldiers, a frightened Peter swore three times he did not know Jesus. Then he remembered Jesus' prediction and was nearly driven to despair for his cowardice. Unlike Judas, the apostle who betrayed Jesus, Peter sorely repented and was forgiven.

Following the Resurrection, Jesus appeared to his apostles. On one such occasion he was by the Sea of Galilee as they were out fishing. Recognizing him, they quickly turned their boat toward the shore. But Peter was too impatient; impulsively he plunged into the water and swam to his master.[5] While all the rest were full of the greatest joy to see Jesus, Peter alone seems to have been driven by his brash heart.

After Pentecost, when the Holy Spirit descended upon the apostles inspiring them to preach the word of God, Peter and the others risked their lives daily going about their master's work. In the Acts of the Apostles we learn that it wasn't long before Peter was imprisoned, but as he lay asleep in his cell, an angel of the Lord came and released him.

The location of Peter and Andrew's house is still marked today. A church was built on the site in A.D. 352. Later it was replaced by a basilica, and excavators unearthed two ancient fish hooks and a small axe for cutting stone. Perhaps the fish hooks and axe belonged to Peter and his brother.

Symbols: keys, cockerel.

Holy days: June 29; modern Anglican churches also celebrate January 18.

Andrew

Today the lush hillsides and blue waters of Galilee are virtually unchanged since Biblical times, when the holy apostle Andrew lived and worked as a fisherman. Andrew was the first apostle whom Jesus chose. His brother was Simon, whom Jesus later renamed Peter.

Interested in the spiritual life, the young Andrew seems to have left his fishing nets to follow John the Baptist. He walked for miles to find this holy prophet preaching at the Jordan River. After Andrew was baptized by the prophet, there came among them seeking baptism, Jesus of Nazareth.

When John the Baptist saw Jesus, he turned the attention of the crowd toward this solitary figure and said, "Behold the Lamb of God..."[6]

Andrew knew that he must seek Jesus out, and he brought his brother Peter, and later Philip to meet Jesus. Though Andrew, Peter, their young cousin John, and Philip were not yet apostles, they accompanied Jesus and his mother to the wedding feast at Cana.[7] There they saw him perform the miracle that changed water into wine. They returned home and took up their trade as fishermen, until Jesus came one day to summon them, saying, "Follow me and I will make you fishers of men."[8]

Andrew took the lad with the five loaves and two fish to Jesus. And he assisted in the distribution of the food once Jesus miraculously multiplied the small provisions so that the crowd of 5,000 would have more than enough to eat.[9] He is listed as an apostle in the Acts of the Apostles; it is the last record we have of him in the New Testament.

Today the apostle Andrew is the patron saint of Scotland; his cross in the shape of an X is the symbol of the country. He is also claimed as patron saint by Orthodox Christians, and of fishermen.

His holy day is celebrated on November 30.

James the Elder

The early church referred to the holy apostle James as "James the Elder" or "James the Great" to distinguish him from "James the Younger" or "James the Less," the son of Alphaeus, who was supposedly a smaller and certainly a younger man. We can imagine James the Elder as a robust, imposing figure, with piercing eyes, a full beard, and a resounding voice that must have commanded respect.

The son of Zebedee, a prosperous fisherman, James was the older brother of John, and a partner of Peter's in business. Jesus called James and John *Boanerges*, meaning "Sons of Thunder" in Greek, for their ardent zeal.[10] Once when the innkeepers in a Samaritan village refused accommodations to Jews, the outraged brothers asked Jesus to call down fire from the heavens to avenge the insult. But Jesus refused, saying, "…the Son of man is not come to destroy men's lives, but to save them."[11]

Holy Scripture describes James, John, and Peter as Jesus' favored apostles; those in his inner circle. Some believe the brothers were the Lord's close relatives and that Peter was their dear friend. These three were present when Jesus raised from the dead the young daughter of Jairus, the synagogue president. They were also with Jesus at the special revelation on the Mount of Transfiguration; and during the long night in the Garden of Gethsemane.

After Pentecost, James' name disappeared from the gospels. Some very ancient traditions dating back to the earliest centuries attempt to explain his absence. It is said that in the years following Jesus' Resurrection James journeyed to Sardinia and Spain to preach the word of the Lord before returning to Jerusalem.

During the Middle Ages the holy apostle James the Elder was one of the most popular figures in Christian Spain, and his patronage was invoked in time of war. His symbol is the sword or the bishop's hat, for he is claimed as the first bishop of Spain.

Holy days: April 30 in the Eastern churches; July 25 in the West.

John the Evangelist

In the Fourth Gospel, John is never mentioned by name, but holy tradition identifies him as the author and anonymous apostle in the text "the disciple whom Jesus loved."[12]

It is further believed that John, son of Zebedee and the younger brother of James the Elder, came from a prosperous family. Like Andrew, John may have been a devoted follower of John the Baptist before becoming Jesus' disciple.[13] With Peter, Andrew, and his older brother, John left his fishing nets when Jesus called them to follow him.

The holy apostle seems to have been one of Jesus' dearest companions. During the Last Supper John sat in the privileged seat at Jesus' right. Later he was present in court at Jesus' trial; perhaps John was permitted because his wealthy family was known to the chief priests.

In Jesus' final hours he called to John from the cross, asking him to take care of Mary, Jesus' mother.[14] As one of the first to see the empty tomb, John's faith was unshakable, for he tells us "…he saw, and believed."[15]

This gentle, humble apostle rose to a position of great respect within the church. Eventually moving from Jerusalem to Ephesus in Asia Minor, he became pastor of the church in that large city, and held influence over other churches in the area. Since the fourth century, there has been a strong belief that John brought Jesus' mother with him to Ephesus, where she remained until her death.

According to tradition John is ascribed the authorship of the Book of Revelations, and three Catholic epistles besides the Fourth Gospel. From these writings we learn that he lived a long life, and thus witnessed and effected the rise of the early Christian era. The last of the twelve to join his master in heaven, legends say John died peacefully in Ephesus at an advanced age in the year A.D. 100.

The holy apostle John is the patron saint of theologians and writers. His symbols are the eagle and the book.

Holy days: in the East, September 26 (also May 8); in the West, December 27.

Matthew

In the Gospel according to Matthew, we are told that Jesus saw a man named Matthew/Levi sitting at the tax collector's booth. "Follow me," he told him, and Matthew got up and followed him.[16]

Tradition suggests that Matthew/Levi, son of Alphaeus, is the brother of the holy apostle James, son of Alphaeus. As a tax collector for the Romans he was regarded as an outcast by his own people. In the first century such officials were often known to be subject to graft and corruption.

In his Miscellanius, Clement of Alexandria tells us Matthew left everything behind to follow Jesus and became a vegetarian, only eating seeds, nuts, and vegetables. Surely it was such faithful devotion that earned him a position as one of the twelve apostles.

After Jesus' Resurrection, Matthew remained in Palestine, preaching in Jerusalem. But a time came when he and the other apostles dispersed to seek converts in distant lands. Before Matthew departed on his missionary journey, tradition suggests that many followers urged this gifted writer to set down from memory the acts and teachings of Jesus. It is said that Matthew fulfilled their request, completing his gospel some eight years after the Ascension of Jesus.

There are many legends of Matthew's ministry to kings and other high government officials. His education in early life and his talent for preaching must have enabled him to present Jesus' teachings to leaders and other influential people in the far-off regions he visited. Early tradition states that he visited Persia and perhaps Macedonia, Syria, Parthia, Media, and Ethiopia.

The holy apostle has frequently been depicted in art with a bag of coins, at a desk with an angel, holding a pen and inkwell, or money box.

Holy days: November 16 in the Eastern churches; and September 21 in the West.

Philip

The name of holy apostle Philip derives from Greek, meaning "he who loves horses." It seems this soft-spoken man had a special relationship with the Greek-speaking Gentiles in the community. When they wanted to meet Jesus, he was approached first. Doubting his own judgment in the matter, Philip turned to Andrew, who took him to tell Jesus of the request.

On the occasion of the miracle of the loaves and fishes to test Philip, Jesus asked him where they would get enough food to feed 5,000. Philip, thinking in practical terms, answered, "Half a year's wages wouldn't buy enough bread for everyone to have a bite."[17]

If as a youthful apostle he lacked confidence, Philip matured, becoming an inspired speaker and healer. After Pentecost, tradition tells that for twenty years he lived and preached in Scythia, and then in Asia Minor at Hierapolis, which in Greek means "Holy City." His sister Miriam and his four daughters joined him in preaching the word of God.

Today Philip's tomb can be found within the ruins of the Turkish city of Hierapolis. There a beneficial mineral spring of warm sparkling water pours forth from the rocks, forming an enormous crystal clear falls that cascades over the side of a mountain, a spectacle nearly as large as the Niagara. In Biblical times it was a famed spa, visited by the sick from all over the Near and Middle East. Looking out at the remains of this ancient city, it is easy to imagine Philip carrying out his ministry with his family. Indeed, legend tells that once the tombs of his daughters, all prophetesses and prominent in the church during the first and early second centuries, could be discovered in Hierapolis as well.

In medieval art Philip's symbol, when not loaves of bread, is a tall cross.

Holy days: in the East, November 14; in the West, May 1—shared jointly with James the Younger; later transferred by the Roman Catholic church to May 3.

Bartholomew

After Philip was chosen by Jesus, he sought out his close friend Bartholomew[18] and told him, "We have found the one Moses wrote about…and of whom the Prophets also wrote— Jesus of Nazareth, the son of Joseph." But Bartholomew said, "Nazareth! Can anything good come from there?" "Come and see," Philip answered. When Jesus saw Bartholomew approaching, he observed, "This man is a true Israelite, in whom there is nothing false." "How do you know me?" Bartholomew asked, and Jesus answered, "I saw you while you were still under the fig tree before Philip called you." Then Bartholomew declared, "Master, you are the Son of God; you are the King of Israel." [19]

Bartholomew is described in *The Apostolic History* of Abdias[20] as a man of middle height with long curly black hair, large eyes, straight nose, and a thick beard. Always cheerful, he had a voice like a trumpet, and knew all languages. Twenty-six years he wore the same white robe with a purple stripe, and a white cloak; yet the garments never tattered or soiled.

Bartholomew's ministry belongs to the tradition of the Eastern churches. He traveled to Asia Minor (Turkey), perhaps in the company of Philip, where he labored in Hierapolis. In the region the ancients referred to as India,[21] it is said that "Bartholomew, one of the Apostles" left behind the Hebrew Gospel of Matthew.[22]

In his long life Bartholomew performed many wonderful feats, including the healing of the sick. With the aid of an angel, he banished from a false idol a demon—described as "sharp-faced, with a long beard, hair to its feet, fiery eyes, breath of flames, and spiky wings."[23] An Apocryphal Gospel of Bartholomew remains to this day.

The Armenian church claims the holy apostle Bartholomew as their founder. In art he is often depicted beside a chained demon; his symbol is a knife blade.

Holy days: in the East, June 11; in the West, August 24.

Jude Thaddeus

The Gospels mention Jude Thaddaeus in the list of the holy Twelve. Sometimes he is called "Lebbaeus," but the Aramaic meaning of Thaddaeus and Lebbaeus is the same, "beloved" or "dear to the heart."

The Fourth Gospel tells us that Thaddaeus asked Jesus, "How is it that you will reveal yourself to us and not to the world?" And Jesus answered, "If a man loves me and obeys my teachings, my father and I will love him and we will come to him and abide with him."[24] Many scholars believe it was the last question Jesus answered before he began his prayer vigil in the Garden of Gethsemane prior to his arrest.

Thaddaeus' esteemed reputation as a miracle-worker may be due to a legend concerning Abgar of Oseoene—the twenty-eight-year-old king of a small, prosperous domain located some 400 miles from Jerusalem. Shortly before Jesus' arrest, the young king wrote to Jesus asking to be cured of a painful disease. Though Abgar never met Jesus, he accepted him as the Savior, and warned that in Jerusalem there were plots against Jesus' life. Abgar offered his own kingdom as sanctuary, saying, "...I have a very small yet noble city which is big enough for us both."[25]

Although Jesus graciously declined the invitation, Abgar was promised that an apostle would be sent to cure him. After the Ascension, Thaddaeus was chosen to travel to Oseoene. He healed the king and many others as well. The legend ends with the grateful Abgar offering Thaddaeus a large sum of gold and silver. But Thaddaeus refused, saying, "If we have forsaken that which is our own, how shall we take that which is another's?"[26]

Since the eighteenth century, Christians in France and Germany have prayed to Jude Thaddeus as the Saint of Lost Causes; today he continues to be petitioned by many Christians throughout the world. His symbol is a gold sailing ship with silver sails before a red horizon.

Holy days: Eastern churches celebrate Thaddaeus on June 19; in the West, with the apostle Simon on October 28.

Simon

The holy apostle Simon is called "the Zealot," [27] perhaps to distinguish him from Simon/Peter. But there is a theory that Simon, along with James the Younger, Jude Thaddaeus, and Judas Iscariot once belonged to the Zealots, a religious sect of "freedom fighters" bitterly opposed to Roman rule over Judea. Some scholars claim that Jesus made certain statements recorded in the Bible of a revolutionary nature that aligned him with members of the Zealot movement. Still others hold that the word "zealot" when referring to Simon merely implied that he was a zealous upholder of the faith.

According to the *Gospel of the Twelve Apostles,* a second-century Apocryphal work, Simon received his call from Jesus while with many of the other apostles at the Sea of Galilee.[28] Yet another account names Simon the bridegroom at the Wedding in Cana, the occasion of Jesus' first public miracle when he turned water into wine at the request of Mary, his mother. In this tradition Simon was so moved by the miracle that he left the wedding festivities and his home to become one of Jesus' apostles. The last mention of Simon is found in the Acts of the Apostles when, following the Ascension, he returned to the city of Jerusalem with the other apostles and Jesus' mother.[29]

The holy apostle is linked with Thaddaeus in the Apocryphal *Passion of Simon and Jude,* which tells of their preaching together in Persia. In the West the two are always joined in the ecclesiastic calendar and in the dedications of churches. An Armenian tradition claims that he preached in Armenia along with Thaddaeus, Bartholomew, Andrew, and Matthias.

The holy apostle Simon's symbol is a book.

Holy days: in the East, May 10; in the West, with Jude Thaddaeus on October 28.

James the Younger

In all four lists of the apostles, James, the son of Alphaeus, is grouped with Thaddaeus, Simon the Zealot, and Judas Iscariot. Scholars speculate that there was a common thread among these men prior to joining Jesus, and that perhaps they all once belonged to the revolutionary religious sect known as the Zealots.

He is sometimes called "James the Younger" or "the Less,"[30] although no significant reason has been found for this, except perhaps to distinguish him from "James the Elder" or "the Great."

It is generally believed that James was the brother of Matthew, since both were sons of Alphaeus. Like his brother, James came from Capernaum in Galilee, on the northwest shore of the Sea of Galilee. Here Jesus came to settle early in his ministry, preaching in the local synagogues, private homes, and on the sandy shores of the sea. Crowds gathered everywhere to listen, and perhaps James came to hear Jesus' teachings in such a way. Though it is supposed that James differed ideologically with Matthew, both brothers were inspired by Jesus. Leaving all else behind, together they put aside their differences and followed him.

One story preserved in the *Golden Legend* relates that James so resembled Jesus that it was difficult for those who did not know them well to tell the two apart.[31] Perhaps there is a small kernel of truth here. Might this be the reason that the kiss of Judas in the Garden of Gethsemane, according to Scripture, was needed? Perhaps it was to make certain that Jesus and not the holy apostle James was arrested. In the apostle James' last days he earned the name the "Divine Seed," for he toiled throughout his life to sow the seeds of Jesus' message. Thus he succeeded in planting faith and goodwill in all who listened.[32]

His symbol is the fuller's club (used in blacksmithing) or a book.

Holy days: in the Eastern churches on October 9; in the West, the Book of Common Prayer *joins him with Philip on May 1; and in the Roman Catholic church, his holy day is May 3.*

Thomas

The holy apostle Thomas is perhaps best remembered as "Doubting Thomas"—the apostle who, when told of the appearance of the risen Christ, declared, "I will never believe it unless I see the holes the nails made in his hands, put my finger on the nailmarks and my hand into his side."[33] Thomas' reaction was certainly practical; perhaps the others overcome with grief were deluding themselves. He had witnessed the tragic death of his beloved master; how was he now to believe that Jesus was alive? Thomas wanted the same astonishing experience as the rest; he wanted proof. When Jesus did appear to him, and Thomas saw the same tortured body that had suffered on the cross, he was overwhelmed, and cried, "My Lord and my God!"[34] Thus Thomas was one of the first to explicitly express Jesus' divinity.

Yet Thomas was not only clearheaded, but brave. During the winter Jesus was forced out of Jerusalem for his teachings. Now, Jesus and his apostles were aware that if he returned, he and perhaps they would be killed.[35] Then a few months later word came that Jesus' great friend Lazarus was gravely ill. The message spoke of illness, but Jesus knew that by the time the news arrived, Lazarus was already dead. Yet Jesus prepared to go to his friend in Bethany, some two miles from the city of Jerusalem, regardless of the risk to himself. Alarmed, the apostles argued against it; why go, they reasoned, if Lazarus was dead? It was Thomas who rallied the others, insisting, "Let us also go, that we may die with him."[36] Here Thomas is not a man of doubt, but of great courage and loyalty.

There are several Apocryphal works that have circulated under Thomas' name.[37] There is much written about his fearless evangelical work and more speculation about his extensive missionary travels than any other of the Twelve. The church of the East and Assyria trace the succession of its bishops back to Thomas. Western India claims him as the founder of the early Christian church.

His symbol is a T square.

Holy days: October 6 in the Eastern churches; July 3 in the West.

Judas and Matthias

Holy Scripture tells us that Jesus knew that both Peter and Judas Iscariot would betray him. Yet Peter repented and, receiving forgiveness, went on to lead the apostles in their ministry as head of the early Christian church. But Judas, though he too later regretted his crime against his master, could not bring himself to seek mercy from the one he had betrayed. Instead, consumed by guilt and grief, he took his own life, thus condemning himself.

The gospels give no clue for his treachery, suggesting only that the betrayer had come to be possessed by evil. The tragic events unfolded in this way: At the time of the Passover feast, the crowds in the city streets of Jerusalem hailed Jesus as a prophet, causing the corrupt chief priests in the Temple to fear for their own position of power. They wanted to be rid of Jesus, but they needed a means that would not enrage the public. Judas Iscariot, for the small price of thirty pieces of silver, showed them the way.

On a clear moonlit night Judas led armed troops to the private Garden of Gethsemane, where Jesus could be captured quietly. Judas arranged to identify Jesus with a signal, thus when he came upon his master, the traitor kissed him, saying, "Rabbi!" Immediately, the troops seized and arrested Jesus. Later Judas tried to give back the "blood money," but the priests refused, turning their backs on him. According to tradition, Judas then flung the silver pieces down and fled. In the end the betrayer hanged himself.

After Judas' death, the holy apostles understood that the fellowship had to be made up to twelve again by appointing someone who had accompanied Jesus throughout his ministry.[38] Two disciples out of the seventy who followed Jesus fit the requirement: Matthias and Barsabbas/Justus. To decide between these good men, sacred lots were drawn for the first time by the apostles, and Matthias was chosen. Some believe that beyond the drawing of lots, a ray of light shone down from the heavens to rest upon Matthias' head, thereby verifying that he was indeed the right choice. Judea was assigned to Matthias, and he preached there and in Armenia, performing many miracles, and went to his eternal rest in peace.

The symbol for Matthias is the ax. Holy days: in the West, Matthias' life is celebrated on May 14; in some Anglican churches, February 24; and in the Orthodox church, August 9.

A Note About this Book ✒

Artists throughout the ages have portrayed Biblical figures in glorious paintings. Perhaps some of the most popular subjects were the Twelve Apostles of Christ. Frequently depicted with symbols—objects or emblems linked to their lives and legends—the Twelve have inspired innumerable masterpieces.

While all the apostles identified in this book are remembered in the New Testament, their legends were found in the Apocrypha and other noncanonical writings. To give a fuller understanding of each apostle's unique personality, legendary tales have been included along with feast days, and specific symbols relevant to each profile.

Acknowledgments ✒

I am deeply in debt to the staff at Super Stock, Art Resource, and the Bridgeman Art Library for their tireless assistance in collecting countless images to choose from. Most particular thanks to Janice Ostan and Simon Taylor.

Also sincere thanks to two friends for suggestions on research material as well as their careful review of the final manuscript: Dan Siemiatkoski formerly assistant manager at Cowley & Cathedral Bookstore in downtown Boston, who is currently pursuing a Ph.D. from Boston College in Theology. And Warren Farha, owner of the bookshop Eight Day Books. The gift of their time and knowledge ensured a more accurate and faithful telling of the material at hand. Thanks also to bookseller Priscilla Bates for her assistance, and to the entire staff at Cowley & Cathedral Bookstore.

Special thanks to assistant editor Amy Goldschlager for her attention to the many details concerning a book of this kind, to say nothing of her cheerful willingness to persevere against the daily challenges presented by the department's color copiers. Her efforts at the early stages of this project helped put together a clear and concise example of the book I envisioned. Praise must also go to my longtime publisher and editor, Phyllis Fogelman. Her unique, unfailing insight and trust have been constant over the many years we have worked together.

Sources & References 🖋

Author's Note
   [1]Matthew 10:40
   [2]Matthew 19:28, Luke 22:30
   [3]Acts 1:16-26

Peter
   [4]Matthew 16:13-19
   [5]John 21:1-8

Andrew
   [6]John 1:29-30
   [7]John 2:1-11
   [8]Matthew 4:18-20
   [9]John 6:1-14

James the Elder
   [10]Mark 3:17
   [11]Luke 9:56

John
   [12]John 19:26
   [13]John 1:34-40
   [14]John 19:26-27
   [15]John 20:8

Matthew
   [16]Matthew 9:9

Philip
   [17]John 6:7

Bartholomew
[18]Also known as Nathanael. He is mentioned as Bartholomew, one of "the Twelve" in Matthew10:3; Mark 3:18; Luke 6:14; and Acts 1:13. There is no further mention in the New Testament. However, John 1:45 refers to him as Nathanael, which has led theologians to believe that Bartholomew and Nathanael are the same person.

[19]John 1:44-51

[20]Bishop of Babylonia ordained by the apostles.

[21]India was used indiscriminately to refer to Arabia, Ethiopia, Libya, Parthia, and the Medes.

[22] Eusebius' *Ecclesiastical History,* Vol. 10:12

[23]*Ibid.*

Jude Thaddaeus

[24]John 14:22-23

[25]*The Apostolic History* of Abdias; see Note 20 re Abdias

[26]*Ibid.*

Simon

[27]Luke 6:15; Acts of the Apostles 1:13

[28]Matthew 4:18-22

[29]Acts of the Apostles 1:13-14

James the Younger

[30]Mark 15:40

[31]*Golden Legend,* Vol. I, p. 270. A two-volume compilation of the lives of the saints.

[32]*Ibid.*

Thomas

[33]John 20:25

[34]John 20:28

[35]John 11:8

[36]John 11:16

[37]The Apocryphal works of Thomas: *Acts of Thomas, Apocalypse of Thomas, Infancy Gospel of Thomas, Book of Thomas,* and the *Gospel of Thomas.*

Judas and Matthias

[38]Acts of the Apostles 1:15-26

List of Illustrations

Albrecht Durer. St. Philip the Apostle. Florence, Italy: Galleria degli Uffizi (Bridgeman Art Library, London), page 14.

Georges de la Tour. Saint Philippe. Norfolk, Virginia: Chrysler Museum (Erich Lessing/ Art Resource, NY), page 15.

Andre Beauneveu. St. Bartholomew, Psalter of Jean, Duke of Berry (c. 1386), Ms Fr 13091 f.22. Paris, France: Biblotheque Nationale (Topham Picturepoint/Bridgeman Library, London), page 16.

El Greco. Bartholomew. Jacksonville, Florida: SuperStock, page 17.

Giovanni Battista Mariotti. Saint Jude. Venice, Italy: S. Stae (Cameraphoto/ArtResource, NY), page 18.

Domenico Fetti or Feti. St. Jude (Thaddeus). Mantua, Italy: Palazzo Ducale (Bridgeman Art Library, London), page 19.

Pascal Dagnan-Bouveret. Study for Simon in "The Supper at Emmaus." London, England: Private Collection/Julian Hartnoll (Bridgeman Art Library, London), page 20.

Carlo Dolci. St. Simon. Florence, Italy: Palazzo Pitti (Bridgeman Art Library, London), page 21

Master of Catherine of Cleves. Saint James Minor (Known for His Abstinence) and a Drinking Scene. Book of Hours of Catherine of Cleves. Netherlands (Utrecht), c. 1435, M.917, p. 224, (the Pierpont Morgan Library/Art Resource, NY), page 22.

Georges de la Tour. St. James the Less. Albi, France: Musee Toulouse-Lautrec (Reunion des Musees Nationaux/Bridgeman Art Library, London), page 23.

Giovanni Toscani. Incredulity of St. Thomas. Florence, Italy: Accademia (Alinari/Art Resource, NY), page 24.

Guercino. The Incredulity of St. Thomas. Vatican State: Pinacoteca, Vatican Museums (Scala/Art Resource, NY), page 25.

Giotto di Bondone. The Betrayal of Christ. Padua, Italy: Arena Chapel, Cappella Degli Scrovegni (SuperStock, FL), page 26

Barent (Bernard) van Orley. Saint Matthew is made a disciple. (Detail from Altar of Saints Thomas and Matthias the Apostle). Vienna, Austria: Kunshistorisches Museum (Erich Lessing/Art Resource, NY), page 27.